Witch's Brew

FOR ME & YOU

WORDS AND PICTURES
BY **DARCEY SHUMAKER**

In memory of my grandmothers,
Carol Booth & Thelma Wood

On Sunday at Nana's, it was storming,
Making this day extra boring.

Nothing to do, nowhere to go,
And time was going oh so slow.

Nana's in the kitchen, cooking away.
She poked her head out to see if I was okay.

"I'm fine, there's just nothing to do!
I've played, I read, I even drew!"

"Why don't you lend a hand a while?
This job is magic," she said with a smile.

"But Nana, you're just making stew!"
She paused, "Oh no, it's witch's brew!

WITCH'S BREW? What could she mean?
That's no ordinary Sunday cuisine!

To the closet, Nana flew
For witches' hats – I get one too!

Pointy and spooky, witchy and dark,
The hats sure give a magic spark!

In the kitchen, we start our task,
"With two of us, this'll go by fast!"

The cauldron (really Nana's pot!)
Bubbles and steams, wicked hot!

We cackle and giggle – as witches do,
Scrubbing potatoes for the stew.

We chop the onions nice and thin,
"Yes, just like that. Then toss them in!"

Now it's time for magic dust,
"They're really spices, always a must!"

Dash and sprinkle, stir and mix,
Using all our witches' tricks...

Peel the carrots, in they go,
With peas and corn, just like so!

Watch the steam curl and coil,
As the mix continues to boil.

While it stews, we slice the bread.
It's soft and warm, a delicious spread!

Set the table, bowls and spoons,
Covered in shiny stars and moons!

I'm so excited, "Is it ready yet?"
"Just one more thing, we mustn't forget!"

"A big thanks for your help," with a hug and a kiss.
"The magic of teamwork is never a miss!"

So now we sit to eat and chat.
We even share some with the cat!

A witch's brew, a yummy stew,
Made with love by me and you.

ABOUT THE AUTHOR

Darcey is an illustrator living in North Carolina with her husband and daughter. Darcey loves to draw cute, whimsical, and cozy things. As a child she frequently got in trouble for drawing too much during school. *Witch's Brew for Me & You* is the first book she's written.

Visit Darcey online at www.darceyshumaker.com
for more info, doodles, and updates on future books.